THE BRAID

THE BRAID

HELEN FROST

THORNDIKE PRESS

An imprint of Thomson Gale, a part of The Thomson Corporation

Detroit • New York • San Francisco • New Haven, Conn. • Waterville, Maine • London

THOMSON
GALE

LIBRARY OF CONGRESS CATALOGING-IN-PUBLICATION DATA

Frost, Helen, 1949–
   The braid / Helen Frost.
     p. cm.
   "Thorndike Press Large Print The Literacy Bridge."
   Summary: Two Scottish sisters, living on the western island of Barra in the 1850s, relate, in alternate voices and linked narrative poems, their experiences after their family is forcibly evicted and separated with one sister accompanying their parents and younger siblings to Cape Breton, Canada, and the other staying behind with other family on the small island of Mingulay.
   ISBN-13: 978-0-7862-9497-8 (large print : hardcover : alk. paper)
   ISBN-10: 0-7862-9497-3 (large print : hardcover : alk. paper)
   1. Large type books. [1. Sisters — Fiction. 2. Family — Fiction. 3. Islands — Fiction. 4. Mingulay (Scotland) — History — 19th century — Fiction. 5. Emigration and immigration — Fiction. 6. Cape Breton Island (N.S.) — History — 19th century — Fiction. 7. Scotland — History — 19th century — Fiction. 8. Canada — History — 1841–1867 — Fiction. 9. Large type books.] I. Title.
PZ7.F9205Bra 2007
[Fic]—dc22
                                               2007000358

Published in 2007 by arrangement with Farrar, Straus and Giroux, LLC.

Printed in the United States of America on permanent paper
10 9 8 7 6 5 4 3 2 1

*Dedicated with love
to my sisters
Mary, Margaret, Kathy,
Barbara, Dorothy, Nancy,
and Karen*

Contents

Introduction

The Braid begins in 1850, near the end of the Highland Clearances, when thousands of people were evicted from the Western Isles of Scotland (also called the Outer Hebrides). The people had lived on the land for many generations, working hard and paying rent, but when it became more profitable for landlords to raise sheep on the land than to collect rent from their tenants, many landlords forced the tenants to leave. Some of the evicted tenants went to cities in mainland Scotland; others went to America, New Zealand, or Australia. Many went to Canada. They were not rich people, and often they did not have time to pack for the journey. Some left home with little more than the clothes they were wearing.

Around that time, the potato crop failed in many places, including both the Isle of Barra, in Scotland, and Cape Breton, in Canada. This caused widespread hunger among people who depended on potatoes for a large portion of their food. The effect was not so severe on the smaller island of Mingulay, to the south of Barra, in part because people there had a more varied diet, including seabirds that nested by the thousands on the island's cliffs.

The Mussel Bailiff
Sarah
Isle of Barra, Scotland, 1850

All of us! Father, Mother, Jeannie, and
    the wee ones — Willie,
Margaret, and Flora — Grandma Peggy,
    and myself. We're all
to be evicted come next Monday. Our
    crime? Nothing more than
hunger: I went with Mother when the
    tide was out, to gather
mussels for our supper. We filled our
    basket. Mother strapped it
to her back. We could hear, from down
    the glen, Old Donald playing
on his pipes, a cheerful tune that Mother
    hummed as wc walked home.
I was happy. We'd have more than
    seaweed in our soup that night.
Then comes the mussel bailiff, so high
    and mighty, like he thinks

13

he is the Duke himself! Him and his
    dogs, all snarling at us —
and he takes out his knife and cuts the
    straps from our basket, so
it falls from Mother's shoulders to the
    mud. He grinds our mussels
underfoot until the shells are just blue
    specks, then tells us we're
to leave our home before this week is out.
    Mussels in that bay,
we're told, are bait for English fishermen,
    not food for Scottish
children like ourselves. If they let one
    family take supper
from the bay, soon everyone, they say,
    will be taking all
the mussels they can eat. *And what,* I
    think, *would be so wrong with that?*
But I know better than to speak such
    thoughts. I hold my tongue.
A ship sits in Lochboisdale now, due to
    sail to Canada
next Tuesday. Father has determined we'll
    all make the journey,
and he's gone to try to sell his tools,
    hoping only that they'll

14

bring enough to pay our passage. It
    troubles me: how will we
build a house in Canada without them? A
    table. Benches.
Willie's cradle. Grandma's loom. A new
    bed for me and Jeannie.
I sit outside with Grandma, knitting.
    We're trying to be good.
Grandma frowns and clicks her needles
    like she's telling them
the thoughts she tries to silence. She's in
    no mood for talking. But
I have so many questions. The day we'll
    leave is coming close.
Who else can I ask? I lean on Grandma's
    shoulder: *How long will*
the journey be? How big is the ship? Will
    there be dogs and cats
in Canada? As I expect, she shushes me.
    She says she
has no answers. I grow silent, breathing in
    the smell of her
wool shawl, the smell of peat smoke and
    the sea, the sour smell where
Willie spat up on her shoulder after
    breakfast. At last she

15

speaks: *Child, my heart is breaking, but I'll*
not be going with you.
I'll take my weaving from the loom and go
back to Mingulay
where I was born. My William's buried in
the graveyard there, and
some days I expect that I may well be there
beside him soon.
Then she takes my head into her hands
and weeps. When she sees tears
on my face, she wipes them with her
fingers, soft and rough at once.
I know she wants to hold me here. I
know too that she'll not try.
She gathers up her tangled wool, takes
her basket back inside.

Mussels

Such beauty in the world, such strength
in all the creatures. Each mussel
somehow finds a rock to cling to,
opening when washed by water,
closing when the tide goes out. Shells
protect the living creature — blue,
black-purple, closed upon the rock,
white inside, shining like the sun.

The Braid
Jeannie
Isle of Barra

Willie fussed, and wouldn't go to sleep. It
    was late, we were
all packed, ready for the journey. Sarah
    held him tighter
than she usually does. She looked long at
    his face and then she
gathered him up, kissed his nose, wrapped
    her shawl around him, pulled
it — pulled Willie — close. She looked at
    Flora, then at Margaret,
playing on the floor with the wee rag doll
    we made for her.
Home, Sarah must have thought.
    Remember this. Later that same
night — we could not sleep — we walked
    together to the cove. Father
thinks that Sarah must have told me then.
    She did not. None of

18

us — not even I — knew what she was
   planning. Sarah was
so quiet. She didn't laugh when an otter
   opened a
mussel with a rock and ate it and I made
   my wee joke:
*We'll tell the bailiff, and he'll send you to
   Canada.* The
bay was still. Moonlight on the water
   made a path from our
Scottish sea to — where? Where, I
   wonder, will we all be eating
supper in two months' time? One year? I
   linked arms with Sarah,
the way we've done since we were small,
   sitting and watching on
that rock. Then we dipped our hands into
   the sea and touched our
tongues to the seawater, each of us
   swallowing a bit.
Canada seemed far away, the salty sea so
   close, our
journey not yet started. We walked back
   home. *Hush now,* Sarah said,
they'll be asleep. So they were, but we
   were wide awake when

we went to our bed. I took the hairbrush
from the wooden
bench, and sat by Sarah, brushing out her
long thick hair. *Oh,*
Jeannie, Sarah whispered. *I can't . . .* She
drew in her breath. Then . . .
Goodnight. (Or did she say *goodbye?*)
She loosened my braids, held
them in her hand, and brushed my hair
so hard — I should have known.
But how could I? Then Sarah braided my
hair with her own,
close and tight, so our heads were
touching. We started laughing.
Will you girls go to sleep? It's near morning!
Father called. Like two
cats curled together, we slept that night.
Or — did Sarah sleep?
She must have stayed awake until I slept.
She must have had
her sewing scissors tucked into her
pocket. Sarah knew
where she was going. I woke to no warm
place beside me.
She'd cut the braid close to our heads,
tucked half into my hand —

You / me / sisters / always.
                  Now we're in the boat,
   and leaving;
Mingulay is but a distant blur. We've left
   without her —
and I want to dive into the sea and swim
   back home. But
soon we will be out too far to see the hills
   where Sarah's
tears are no doubt falling like my own. I
   squeeze my right hand
once, around the braid in my pocket.
   Father says, *Be strong.*
Try to be as helpful as you can. Your
   mother needs you.
Inside, I'm still crying. *I'll hold Margaret's*
   hand, I say.

Hair

White, shining in the sun, Grandma's
hair winds round her head, a braid, a
crown. Margaret's hair, black and fine,
damp on her cheek in fretful sleep.
Flora's and Jeannie's golden curls,
Sarah's red-brown braid — Mother's strong
hands, teasing out the tangles as
she sings into her children's ears.

After Three Days
Sarah
Isle of Barra

Were they angry? Could they understand
   how this place holds me, so
tight I could not live away from it? Nor
   could I leave Grandma.
She scolded, but she was pleased when,
   after three days, my hunger
pulled me back here. That first day, I hid
   and watched their boat go out —
Margaret kneeling at the bow, arms
   spread like a bird. Behind
her, Mother, strong and watchful, one
   hand upon her shoulder, the
same way she watched me when I was
   four. Flora sat straight beside
Father. Jeannie held Willie. No doubt she
   sang to him. Boxes
of food for the journey, and two other
   men — the fishing boat

was full. A man named Ranald took them
    to Lochboisdale. He has
a younger brother going to Canada by
    choice. Jeannie
joked: *He should go in place of one of us*
    — perhaps now she thinks
the joke has turned out true.
                    Grandma tells me about
    Mingulay:
*Our life will not be easy. We'll have fish and
    birds and eggs to*
*eat; I have no fear of starving. But winters
    can be long — and*
*Sarah, only twenty families live there. You'll
    be lonesome*
on your own. She looks hard at me. *I'll
    have you,* I say. She blinks.
*Our journey there is likely to be rough.
    Some say it's every*
bit as daunting as the trip to Canada . . .
    Well, then. We link
our arms and walk down to the cove.
    Sarah's coming, too, Grandma
says to Murdo Campbell, the young
    fisherman who's taking us.
When he sees me, arm in arm with

Grandma Peggy, clutching my
wooden walking stick like it's my sister, I
    can't guess his thoughts.
Oh, Sarah, don't you worry, now, Grandma
    Peggy says. (I know,
then, I should be worried.) *If anyone can
    land a boat or*
*hold us steady in a stormy sea, it's Murdo
    Campbell. He's*
*known for landing safely on Mingulay when
    others can't.* My
own thoughts I keep to myself: Have I
    been foolish? Is this man
laughing at me? I know my hair must
    look odd where I cut it;
two patches on my skirt are coming
    loose; the past three nights I've
slept out in the hills, with little food.
    Here, Murdo says, *I*
*had two old waterproofs at home, and
    brought them both. You'd think I*
knew that you were coming, Sarah. I take
    the small one. He looks
me up and down as if he's weighing me,
    then shifts his anchor,
hands me a bailer — *just in case* — seats

Grandma Peggy to his
left, me to his right, and pushes us out to
    sea. Grandma folds
her hands and bows her head. I look up
    at Murdo — his eyes calm,
but merry, arms pulling hard on the oars.
    He looks at me. *Aye,*
Sarah, they'll be glad, on Mingulay, to have
    a lively lass.
Hand me that parcel, would you? He
    opens it and offers me
strong tea, still hot, and a hard-boiled
    egg. *The birds are calling to*
you, he says, pointing overhead: gulls
    circling, screeching. If they
say anything, it's likely, *You, there —*
    where do you think you're going?

Song

The songs that enter children's ears
carried across centuries of
love, stay with them, bringing comfort,
setting their feet dancing, coming
back to them when their own children
first look up and see them smiling
or hear them weeping as they rock,
strong boats upon a stormy sea.

Going On Without Sarah
Jeannie
Crossing the Atlantic

So many people in so small a space. This
    ship is like
Grandma's salted herring, people packed
    that tight, everyone
hungry, cranky, some sick — a man died
    yesterday. I go
out to the windy upper deck, taking
    Willie, leaving
behind our crowded sleeping quarters
    down below. That air —
the stench of it won't leave my hair and
    clothes. Last night I slept
beside Margaret. She was thirsty, so I
    climbed over
boxes, stepped around people, to the
    water by the life-
boat. Even the water stinks. Father
    wonders if the ship

28

has enough water to last the crossing. He
    cautions me:
*Jeannie, let's try not to drink too much too
    soon.*

Always, I'm
thinking about Sarah. Is she thirsty? Did
    she go to
Mingulay with Grandma? Or is she still
    hiding, frightened
to come down from the hills, but hungry
    where she is, alone
and cold at night? Sarah's strong and
    clever, and yet . . . Oh, I'm
lonesome for her. So is Mother — she
    bites her bottom lip and
blinks back tears whenever someone
    mentions Sarah. And is
everyone expecting me to take her place?
    I can't! I
link arms with Flora, as Sarah used to do,
    but it's like
Grandma trying to act like Mother. *Why
    did Sarah leave
us, Jeannie?* Flora asks. She's six years
    old — her question is
my question, too, and only Sarah has the

answer. Our

thoughts of Sarah stretch from here to
her like yarn unwinding.

Know this, Jeannie, Mother says, as if she
fears that yarn could snap,

or trip someone — as if she can see my
thoughts unravel —

*she's not lost to us. She'll always be our
Sarah. But now,*

*my Jeannie, you'll be the oldest and we'll
count on you.* (A

man walks by and looks at us. Do I look
older? Or is

it my short hair he's staring at — is he
laughing at me?

I glare at him — he turns away.) Though
I'm the oldest *here,*

I'm not at all like Sarah! Compared to
her, I'm useless.

I've never stood by Father as he works,
the way Sarah

looked on, learning how to use his tools,
or when to pull the

anchor when we went out fishing. *Just
like a lad,* he'd say,

his eyes twinkling. As if a lad is better

than a lass!

Fold these dry clothes, will you, Jeannie?
Mother, usually so
calm, seems fretful. I study her. *Is
something wrong?* I ask.
*Aye, Jeannie — it's Margaret. She's taken
ill. The poor wee
lass was up all night. She can't keep her
food down. It worries
me.* I jump up — *I'll do this later, Mother!*
I go down
to Margaret, hot and sweaty, asleep in
Father's lap.
They both look dreadful, and Father
won't let me stay to help.
Go back up to your mother. Now! he barks.
My blood goes cold.

Boats

A strong boat on a stormy sea,
blackened by tar that seals its joints,
rises on every cresting wave,
rides down again into each trough. Swell
of the water, curve of the boat,
swift mind of the oarsman who knows
the shape of each rock, each island.
Knows the way into the harbor.

Stormy Evenings, Dancing
Sarah
Mingulay, Scotland

Like a puffin returning to her nest,
    Grandma has come home.
Everyone here loves her, and because I'm
    hers, they welcome me.
Go ask your aunt if she has oil to spare,
    Grandma says. When I
leave, Aunt Mairi gives me a plucked
    kittiwake. *Something more than*
air and water for your supper. It's eighteen
    days now since I
slept in my bed with Jeannie. Their
    journey is nearly halfway
over; they'll soon be in Canada — as they
    move towards that
life, will they be forgetting me? Last night
    I dreamed about their
ship, a dark cloud above it, Jeannie all
    alone, crying for

33

me. I reached out to her, but woke before
    she took my hand.
I'm fretting about all of them. Grandma
    tells me I should try
to put it from my mind. She hands me a
    broom. *Sarah, why be*
frightened about things you cannot know?
    You know your sister's not
alone. I start to sweep. She watches me.
    Nor are you, she adds.

I have cousins here I don't know well.
    Aunt Mairi's sons, Angus
and James — Angus is about my age (he's
    just turned sixteen); James
is eight, trying hard to be as much like
    Angus as he can.
I go with them to the cliff top to gather
    seabirds' eggs. I'd
like to learn to snare the birds, but
    Grandma says, *No, Sarah, you*
leave the birding to the boys. I don't see
    why.
                    Murdo Campbell
is still here, waiting for the sea to calm.
    We're lucky we made

our landing here the day we did, he says.
  He sits with the men,
unwinding tangled lines, barking the nets
  and sails. When his line
snaps, he doesn't snap at it, as I often do
  if a sock
unravels while I'm knitting. I've grown
  used to Murdo's teasing —
now when he jokes about my hair, I tease
  him right back. He has
a merry laugh; I like to hear it. These
  stormy evenings, there
is dancing at Aunt Mairi's house, and
  Murdo often chooses
me to be his partner — out of kindness, I
  suppose. Others
here have known him longer, and are
  prettier by far than I.
Useless, anyway — soon the weather will
  clear and he will leave.

Sarah, Murdo says, *the sky is clearing. I'll
  be leaving in*
the morning. I carry an armload of his
  nets; we walk, not
saying much. At his boat, he lifts the nets

35

from my arms. *You're a*
lass I'll not be soon forgetting. Like a lad in
    some ways, yet
so . . . delightful — oh, that hair! He
    smiles, reaches out to touch it.
(*Ask if he'll return,* I tell myself, but I do
    not.)
                                        In the
wee hours of the next morning, I wake as
    I often do, with
worries — Mother, Father, Jeannie, Flora,
    Margaret — I go
down the list to Willie and find, like the
    braid I hold in my
lap, a new name wound in with the
    others: *Murdo.* I go to
help him launch his boat, but I'm too
    late. Already, out on the
cold and restless sea, I see his boat, him
    pulling hard away.

Dreams

In dreams we harbor what we know
and almost know and briefly see
between our sleep and waking. A
falling tree, a wolf track, a white
horse walking forward. A woman
wearing a white dress stands beside
an old house, smiling — *welcome.*
  Dreams
surface like seals, dive deep, swim far.

The Crossing
Jeannie
Quebec City, Canada

Home: it seems so far away and long ago.
  Mother tells
me not to think about the brutal crossing,
  but how can
I forget the sickness spreading through
  the hold, each day worse
than the day before, and nothing we
  could do to stop it?
I held Margaret. She shivered. She would
  not eat or drink.
Halfway across the sea, she died. Our
  sweet Margaret. And
that was only the beginning. Father and
  Mother spoke
their prayers, I sang a lullaby, we gave up
  her body
for the sea to take away. Then Flora.
  Father put his

hand on her hot forehead, and ordered
    me away. *Go now!*
Try to keep Willie warm and dry. Did
    Father know he might
be dying too? That night he said, *Jeannie,*
    help your mother.
Not gruff, as he could be — something
    tender in the way he
added, *There's more to you than we've yet*
    seen. If I'd only
known — those were Father's last words
    to me. That night — we had just
sixteen days of our journey left — Father
    and Flora both —
can it be? — died while Mother, Willie,
    and I slept. Now when
I try to sleep, I can't. I'm crying for them
    — and Sarah.
You bring me comfort, Jeannie, Mother
    says. I don't see how.
Why am I here? What will we do? How
    will Mother and I
make a home in Canada alone? Who will
    help us? A
man whose wife and son died on the
    crossing stood with us in

line as we got off the ship. Alone like us,
  he picked up Willie's
sock when it fell off, and then — he
  asked to marry Mother!
Teasing or sincere? (Mother simply said,
  No, thank you.) We
have a bit of money sewn into our skirts
  — but not much.
There is nothing — no one — for us
  here. Mother has made a
choice — we're going to Cape Breton,
  where we hope we might find
others from home who went there more
  than twenty years ago.
I wonder — will we find them? Mother
  was a girl when they
left — will they know her? Will they help
  us if they do? We get
in another line. People move away, as if
  we are
not good enough, or clean enough, to
  speak to. Willie has
a runny nose, and won't stop crying. I
  know how he feels,
yet I feel something else as well here —
  like a baby seal,

it pops its head up from the ocean of my
   grief, peers through
the terror of the crossing. I look around
   at people
with clean clothes, parcels tied with
   string, who know where they are
going, and I feel — hope. How is that? I
   have nothing but
my mother, my brother, and the ragged
   dress I'm wearing
to this new place, Cape Breton. Yet I have
   my life. I have
the one thing so many others lost. No
   one will take that
away. Somehow, somewhere, I will make
   of it what I can.

Seals

Seals dive deep, swim far, surfacing
wherever watchers don't expect
them. Look, there — a black head
     bobbing
in the water by that rock. Round
eyes stare at us — dark, unblinking.
Seals sing, or cry, or bark, or none
of those — that low voice all their own,
mysterious, inside the wind.

Part of the Island
Sarah
Mingulay

Tell me, Sarah, Grandma Peggy sighs, *why
     must you always —* I
can guess she'll say — *do everything the
     boys do?* She claims that I'm
worse here, away every morning with my
     cousins to the cliffs.
It is hard to snare the seabirds, but I'm
     learning. Now Grandma
drinks her tea as I tell her how I reach
     down from the cliff top
and slip my noose around a shag, pull it
     tight, catch the bird! I
speak with such excitement she does not
     outright forbid it. My
body aches all over. *You're so like your
     father,* Grandma says.
*His arms could be near falling off, and he
     would keep on fishing.*

43

Now she's found a pair of Grandpa
    William's trousers, thinking she
might take them in to fit me. *You'll be*
    safer wearing these. Your
mother would not want you clambering
    around those cliffs in skirts.
He — Grandpa William — was a large
    man, and Grandma Peggy can
only do so much with thread and scissors.
    So it is that I'm
just back from birding, dressed like an
    old man, guillemots in
both my hands, hair grown back a bit,
    but wild as the cliff-top wind —
when Murdo Campbell comes again. He
    laughs. My face grows hot. *Oh,*
Sarah, not to worry! You're more a lass
    than ever. I see
how you've this island in you now, he says.
    We walk to the cove.
I let the sea foam wash my feet beside a
    line of shells. Like
a necklace on the sand, they are: pink,
    blue-black, gold, some with life
inside them, one round white one, a star
    at its center, small as

Willie's fingernail. I hold them in my
    hand and recall my
mother's smile, her strength. How are the
    tiny shells not ground to sand?
We climb to the cliff top, raucous with
    kittiwakes and gulls, so
much swooping out, flying in! Murdo
    reaches his arm into
a puffin's burrow — we have seen the
    puffin fly away — and
finds an egg. He holds it out for me —
    most likely laid not long
ago. I take it: cream-colored, with streaks
    of violet-brown.
They're pointed on one end like this — he
    touches it — *so if they*
get too close to the cliff's edge, they won't
    roll off. The two of us
are standing near the cliff's edge,
    breakers pounding below, where they
have crashed through the arch into that
    sea cave forever. The egg
feels fragile in my hand — I put it in my
    pocket. A lone
seal bobs in the sea, dives, and comes up
    some distance off. It looks

through the salty haze, as if gazing
straight at us. *Seals are like
people,* I say. *I know they often swim
alone, but I think
they're happier together.* Murdo looks
thoughtful, says, *Perhaps,
but when you spend your life alone at sea,
you grow used to it.*
Wearing an old gray-blue jacket, Murdo
smiles at me, and I
have trouble separating his eyes from the
gray-blue sea. In
that moment, something sudden makes
me turn my face away. We
can see for miles. We're both quiet as we
turn to go back home.

Wind

Mysterious, inside the wind —
the seeds and sand, all the unseen
fragrances. Rain slashing down, fire
flaring up, sails billowing, clouds
forming, flying, fading. A girl's
hair whips hard around her face. Does
she hear a distant bagpipe? Or an
owl? *No, it's only me,* says Wind.

Alone Among These Giant Trees

Jeannie
Cape Breton, Nova Scotia

I see an otter sliding down a muddy
    riverbank.
I'm comforted a bit — one small familiar
    face. The sea
cliffs here are hidden behind dark forests.
    I remember
Grandma telling of a forest she once
    heard about — tree-
tops higher than houses — we thought it
    was a fairy tale.
I see now, such trees are real — they rise
    up all around us!
My eyes long to rest on a wide and empty
    sky. These trees
say to us: *You're small. You're nothing.*
        We have found no home here.
Fishing, picking berries, we stay alive, but
    Mother's weak.

She still believes we may find our kin; I
    don't expect to.
Your kin may have gone to Australia, one
    man told us. Our
skirts are torn and dirty. We sleep in any
    shelter we
can find — an old barn when it rains, the
    forest when it's clear.
I see tracks of animals — large, unknown
    to me. I peer
into the trees and listen hard — a wolf?
    An owl? Or the
wind? I shiver and hold Willie tight.
    People stare at us —
Oh, I miss Sarah! She'd know how to
    make a home! But I
see no way to fetch her, and we cannot
    return.
                        A wee
cove near here is our best source of water
    — a flat rock is
like a table. We've learned to dig into the
    sand for clams.
Life sometimes feels safe on mornings
    when the weather's clear. Then,
as a storm comes in from the distance, I

must gather all
my courage — speaking to strangers is, to
    me, like eating
sand, but we have to ask for shelter and a
    bit of food.
So we trudge along a dirt road, hungry
    and tired. I look
into a farmyard where a farmer tries to
    shoo a pig
and chickens into a pen. *Might we have an
    egg?* I ask.
Long and hard he stares at us — at me —
    my skirt crusted with
brown dirt, holes in both my shoes. He
    glances at his chickens —
they have all but one escaped. He looks
    around, then back at
us. *Where is the baby's father?* Tears
    spring to my eyes;
they fall before I stop them, and he holds
    up one precious
egg — *here* — and smiles at me. He sees
    that Mother and I are
alone and says, *Come with me, miss. I'll
    show you where you might
look for eggs.* Mother takes Willie from

me then — we do not
like this man. We walk away. We both fall
    silent.
                                    Do you
think . . . Mother . . . (Are there words for
    such a question?) *Do you think*
perhaps he thought . . . that I am Willie's
    mother? My cheeks burn.
It did appear that way, she answers. And
    then: *Oh, Jeannie,*
I see great beauty coming to you. She
    looks intently
into my face — is she complimenting me?
    Warning me?
I cannot tell. Thunder (beauty?) rumbles
    in the distance.
Home seems farther off than ever. I take
    one step. One more.

Owl

Snowy owl, silent in the wind
as evening comes on, glides past
people walking home from working
all day in the field, bringing in
the harvest. In her talons, she
too carries food, a lemming for
her owlets waiting in the nest.
She feeds them, smooths her feathers,
    rests.

This Secret
Sarah
Mingulay

Banking the fire before I go to bed, I
    listen to the
sea, the wind, a distant tune from Uncle
    Allan's bagpipes. I
remember a song he and Aunt Mairi sang
    one evening: two
trees in a churchyard, branches twined
    above the lovers' graves, a
tale of love that lasts beyond this life.
    Hearing that, I thought: *Like*
us, that love — like Murdo and myself.
    We'll be like those two strong
trees, roots deep, growing close together.
    Oh, I wish Jeannie were
here — I want to tell this secret, whisper
    and laugh until we're
weak (or Father shushes us). *A young man*
    cares for me. I have

53

to tell someone! Murdo whispered
    something to me — is this love?

Our time together was too short, three
    days and four short evenings.
We both hoped that — like last time he
    was here — the storms would not
    soon
clear. Grandma tried hard to keep me
    busy; whenever I came in, she
peered at me. Before she could ask
    questions, I'd go out to stack
the peat or pluck the seabirds. Evenings,
    at the ceilidh, she watched
us dance — I know she likes Murdo; is
    she a bit surprised that
I have caught his eye? All my life, it has
    been Jeannie — or our
wee Flora — that people fuss about.
    Their curly yellow hair
is prettier than mine, and Jeannie's always
    smiling, while I
clam up when people speak to me. Yes, I
    miss my sister, but
then I wonder — if she were here with
    me, would Murdo be like

all the rest, drawn to her, while I was lost
   in Jeannie's shadow?
Eating supper — a kittiwake I caught —
   Grandma sets down her
food and remarks about the feathers we
   are saving. *Sarah,*
look at these — one day, we'll have enough
   for a feather bed. She's
trying, in her way, to say, *When you're*
   ready to be married —
asking no harsh questions, but
   suggesting: *That will not be soon.*
(With not enough feathers for a pillow,
   and almost all the
seabirds away now for the winter.)
                    Murdo is, I trust, safe
at home on Barra. I'm out here
   remembering his gray-blue
eyes. My family must have crossed to
   Canada by now — so
precious to me . . . and so far away. I am
   uneasy: Where
are they sleeping? Have they enough
   food? Has Father built a house?
Might Jeannie be as tall as Mother now?
   Is Willie walking?

(Not yet, I think, but likely crawling all
      about.) *Jeannie, do*
you have our braid? I take my half out of
      my pocket, and I
think of everyone I love, watching the
      fire's soft glow as it
burns low. Mother and Father won't
      know about Murdo; he and
Jeannie will not meet. I loosen the braid,
      spread it in my lap,
intent on picking out a sprinkling of
      shells — when Murdo touched
my hand, I was holding them; I dropped
      them in my pocket. From a
distance, no one would have known he
      whispered, *I'll return. We'll have*
more time together. I replied, *May you be*
      safe until then.

Feathers

Feathers, smoothed through fingers, rest
     on
a young girl's open hand: strong spines,
soft edges, nearly weightless — one
breath carries them into the air.
Above, on a gannet's wingtips,
feathers guide the flight, the sudden
plummet from a high and cloudless
sky, to the water, to the fish.

Like This Black Spider
Jeannie
Cape Breton

The days grow colder. People tell us there
     will soon be snow.
I don't know how we will survive. Our
     clothes are wearing thin.
Two nights ago we slept outside, curled
     close together in
a haystack; when we woke, our hair was
     white with frost. *Be*
like this black spider, I try to tell myself.
     Find something
strong within yourself. Climb it. Spit out
     more. Late last night we
were lucky to find this barn to sleep in.
     Now it's morning.
We hope the rain will let up so our damp
     clothes can dry. We
have no money left. We must find food
     today. All those who

love us are in Scotland — it is strangers
    we must ask each
evening for the simple kindness of a place
    to sleep.
Soon the girl will come in to milk the
    cow. If we're lucky,
she will give us each a cup of milk. I will
    offer to
stack their wood, clean out their
    henhouse, fetch water, or maybe
watch the baby so the mother can go
    about her chores.
That is how we have been getting by all
    summer, trading
our help for food and shelter, washing
    out our clothes and
hair in lakes and rivers. But when the
    lakes and rivers freeze?
I shudder when I think of that.
                The barn door creaks open,
but it is not the young girl I saw when we
    arrived. I
liked her; she seemed kind. This must be
    that girl's mother, with dark
shadows under her eyes. Her hands are
    cracked and red. *Be gone!*

(Her voice so tired — angry.) *We've not
    enough to feed ourselves!*
(Sarah. What would Sarah do?) *There's
    thousands of you starving!*
(She's kicking straw at us!) *Missy, you be
    careful who you
marry!* I don't know why she's shouting
    that . . . I back away.

Soon we're walking down the road again.
    Willie is heavy.
The sky looks clear in the distance, near
    the sea. Is there some
safe harbor for us somewhere? We keep
    walking until the
gray-blue of the sky meets the dark blue
    sea. It reminds me
so of home. A noisy crowd has gathered
    along a dock
where a ship is full of food. A man shouts
    out, *I have a
house full of hungry children!* The captain
    hears but keeps on
walking up and down the deck. He
    shouts, *What would you have me
do? What shall I tell my bank?* He's almost

pleading with us.
I can't let them starve, says the man. The
   captain drops his hands.
It's as if he wants to feed us all — but
   how? I move up
and try to get a better look, sit down to
   watch. In my
lap, Willie squirms to crawl away, after a
   dead bird he sees. *Don't*
touch! I say. I look at the captain. He sees
   me watching.
A long moment passes. He turns, steps
   down, opens up the hold —
Have what you need, he tells us all. His
   crew stares open-mouthed.
Then the captain brings a bag of oats,
   puts it in my arms.

Food

Water from the sky and two fish
from the water. A slice of bread,
half a bucketful of berries.
So we are nourished, so we move
forward, finding in each day food
to carry us beyond that day.
From trees: red apples, purple plums.
From the ground: potatoes, carrots.

Almost Like Sisters
Sarah
Mingulay

Snow quiets us and draws us close to one
    another. Outside, a
thin wail of wind tries to get inside, but it
    does not. All our tracks,
in and out, house to house, are quickly
    covered. Grandma Peggy has
been ill, and today she's stayed in bed,
    knowing I'm here if she needs
something for her cough. She is sleeping
    now. Aunt Mairi has come by.
We sit by Grandma's bedside drinking
    tea, steam rising from our cups.
Morning stretches long. We fall into
    stories — almost like sisters,
we talk on. Aunt Mairi tells me that I
    often make her think of
who my father was at my age: *Sixteen
    when he left Mingulay.*

Each day that winter, he grew more
*   restless, until he could barely*
sleep. That spring — it came late that year
*   — he went to live on Barra.* How
lucky they were that Father was a
    fisherman, and strong. He could row
    home
to see them. Aunt Mairi tilts her head,
    studies me. What does she see?
Maybe she knows, although I seem
    cheerful as I go about my
chores, I ache with longing for my family.
    Do you wish you could
trade places with your sister? she asks. *No,*
    I answer, *this is home*
and I am glad of that. But — what I
    cannot say to her: Something
freezes in me when I think of them. I
    almost see them through an
open window — they are not happy —
    then the window closes, and
I feel like I am barefoot in the snow,
    wandering outside, some
dark place where no one knows me. The
    feeling passes; after it has
gone, I start to cook — potatoes, dried

birds, bannocks, bread — more than
we,
ourselves, can eat. I cook as if I am afraid
the old times of
starving will return, and it is up to me
alone to feed us.
You'll always long for Jeannie, Aunt Mairi
says. *No matter how far*
away she is, you may know when
something hard is happening to her.
Heavy words, to know there is something
but not know what. Some deep well,
some knowledge I can't name, sends
pictures to me. I take a deep breath.
The troubling part, I say, *is in what I do not*
see. If you ask
me who is yet alive, and who is not, I
cannot say. (A ship
docks — somewhere — in the shape of a
coffin. Is this a vision or
a fretful dream?) Aunt Mairi only nods.
She rests a steady hand
on my shoulder as she pours another cup
of tea. It comforts
me, though she is neither Jeannie nor my
mother. If Grandma hears

us talking, she doesn't show it, apart from
   a flutter of her
hands and a short cough when our talk
   takes a turn and Aunt Mairi brings
up the subject of "a certain red-haired
   fisherman." When she sees
my face flush, Aunt Mairi says, *Be a little
   careful. You're still young.*
Don't be too quick to give your heart away.
   I nod, but think, *Too late,*
watching what I say, in case Grandma is
   listening. Some dreams I
hold in a safe place. If one touch and a
   few sweet words from Murdo's
mouth at our farewell are all it takes to
   start me thinking of his
arms around me, I know enough to keep
   such daydreams to myself.

Potatoes

From the ground, each round potato,
russet, brown, or gold — crumbs of dirt
still clinging to its skin — just fits
into the palm of the hand that
pulled it from the earth. Brushed clean
     and
roasted, held again in two hands,
it offers warmth, then nourishes
the body, the hands that held it.

Looking
Jeannie
Cape Breton

A rusty saw blade, seven nails, two shells,
    a flat stone — large
tracks by the river make me take stock of
    all these things I
have gathered, in hopes that they might
    help us make a home here.
Need has made me bold. Mother and I
    built a rough shelter
by leaning branches against fallen logs,
    but this morning,
cups of water in the shelter are covered
    with ice. My
sister is not here, so it is me trying hard
    to think
of some way we can stay warm. When
    Father was a boy on
Mingulay, he helped his father build a
    solid stone house,

barely big enough for their family. And
   once he saw
how to do it, he made our own larger
   house. These days, that
home seems long ago, far away. Yet, in my
   mind, I still
see Father pick up each stone, turn it
   over, study it.
My bits and pieces are like those stones,
   and I study them.
Could I find a way to use these things
   I've found to make a
home for Mother, Willie, and myself? If I
   keep thinking,
some idea will surely come. So it is that
   when we pass
an old shed in the corner of a wheat field,
   weathered gray
and reeking of rotten potatoes, I
   somehow see: *our home.*
A man is whistling as he walks toward it
   with a torch. He
has packed dry straw around it — he
   means to light it on fire!
We'll clean out your shed! Don't burn it! We
   need a place to live!

Of course he thinks I have gone mad. He
    stares at us, then shoos
us off, ignores us. Are we nothing more
    than pesky flies?
Far across the field, I see his house. I see
    a woman,
her dress bright blue and white, coming
    toward us. Some small hope
wells up. The man lights his torch, raises
    it. I draw in my
breath, grab the flaming torch, and throw
    it on the ground. I don't
ask permission. All that has happened
    since we boarded the
ship comes over me — I stomp on his
    torch as if it's death
or hunger, as if I could extinguish them
    with my own
hands and feet. The woman arrives, looks
    at us. It's him she'll
comfort, I've no doubt, and they'll send
    us away. But when she
hears what I have offered, she smiles —
    says my plan sounds good to
her! The man shakes his head, then looks
    at her, at us, and nods. They

bring us a bucket, a shovel, point out a
    nearby stream. I
see the enormity of what we've taken on.
    (Two girls,
younger than myself, run by holding their
    noses.) We work
late into evening, shoveling the slimy
    mess outside.
I know it will take days. The smell will
    linger. But then — a
place to stay dry! For Mother to sew. For
    Willie to take
his first steps — most likely any day now.
    And what about
myself? A place to sleep and, upon
    waking, look ahead.

Stones

The body of the earth holds stones
of every size, spits them out
at random. A seeker somehow
finds the perfect stone, exactly
the right shape and size to fit each
space in a wall, the stones to form
each door, each window. The way each
word comes forth and finds its way home.

Around the Rocks
Sarah
Mingulay, 1851

Large storm clouds loom in the distance.
    Whitecaps roughen the nearer sea.
I've come with James and Angus to the
    cliffs. Birds are coming back — *look*
here — a pair of puffins meets after six
    months out at sea. They take
shelter together in their burrow. I
    remember Murdo, that
morning when we walked together and he
    gave me a puffin egg.
My eyes scan the sea — though I know
    it's too rough for him to come. I
think I see a gannet dive and catch a fish
    and eat it, rocking
on the waves. James has caught three
    guillemots. Now he turns toward his
house. We all decide to get back home
    before the storm comes. I

see Aunt Mairi rushing up here to meet
her boys. No — it appears
that it's me she's looking for. *A boat is
coming,* she whispers. *I
still don't know for sure who's here, but
perhaps you want to come and watch.*
It doesn't take us long to hurry to the
landing place. I tell
them, *In this weather, our help will be
needed.* Uncle Allan takes
a rope and their pony to help pull in the
boat. I crane my neck,
thinking — yes — it *is* Murdo (and
someone else with him) coming in,
passing around the rocks — they should
be safe now — just ahead of the
gray bank of clouds. The rain starts just
as they land — he's barely made it
home before the storm. (*My home, not
his. He's been gone for seven months.
He may not have been thinking about you,*
I warn myself.) But this
fire in my heart is not so easy to
extinguish when, in real
life, not a daydream, Murdo steps from
his boat.

What's wrong? Why are his
shoes more interesting than I am? He
    won't look my way. Everyone
flies around, pulling up the boat,
    chattering, laughing. *(He loves a*
woman back on Barra. He has come to tell
    me, so I will not
hope.) The fisherman who came with
    Murdo looks at me, studying
my face. *Are you Sarah MacKinnon? I'm*
    Ranald Macintosh. I
don't believe we've met. Does his face,
    too, hold something dark? Is he not
the man who took my family to their
    ship? (That image — someone's
death — the coffin ship.) I look away
    from him. And from Murdo. My
own face will show no more than his. If
    he does care for another,
she'll not need to hear of me. And what
    Aunt Mairi no doubt guesses,
she will, I trust, not tell. All these
    thoughts go through my mind on the
    way
to Uncle Allan and Aunt Mairi's house. If
    they see I'm quiet,

they say nothing, and when everyone goes
  inside, I slip away.
I go home and sit beside the fire, hold the
  braid, and think of two
girls laughing together when we went to
  sleep, or singing while we
worked. *(Where are you tonight, Jeannie? I
  wonder if you think of me.)*
Outside, the storm breaks over us, as
  Uncle Allan starts to play
a bagpipe tune, a soft strathspey. I hear in
  his music: *Sarah,*
take your time, then come and join us.
  Whatever Murdo's silence is
about, whatever news I do not wish to
  hear, the only way
ahead of me is out this door, through the
  rain, toward the others.

Puffins

How do puffins find their way home?
Like people gathered for a feast,
they fly in from the sea, return
home to their island cliffs each spring.
Nesting in deep burrows, each pair
tends one chick — see how they carry
fish in their bright beaks, head to tail,
like children in a crowded bed.

Shipbuilders
Jeannie
Cape Breton

Sea-wind here reminds me of the wind
    on Barra. When I go
looking for driftwood for our fire, the
    wind blows right through me. I
take what wood I can carry, and hope it
    burns long enough so
that I'll get warm before I must go out
    for more. We can cook
eggs and fish and bannocks on a flat
    stone heated on the fire.
I'm thinking about how I could make
    furniture: a bed, a
rocking chair, a table, or a simple bench.
    Willie straddles
his "horsie" — a three-foot-long log I
    rolled home and brought inside.
I chuckle when he whinnies like a horse,
    and Mother says, *It*

appears that Willie is as clever as his sister.
Of course
I assume she is talking about Sarah, but I
    see her
watching me, thinking, and she adds, *I*
    mean you — I don't need to
tell you that, do I?
                    I've found a place, a
    mile away, where I
take wood from the scrap heap of a
    shipyard. *Jeannie, you'll break your*
neck, Mother tells me, *carrying those*
    heavy pieces of wood
in your small arms. But I'm stronger than
    she thinks. I'm happy when
the shipbuilders make errors: a curved
    hull, miscut — they can't use
it — and I see: a table leg. I drag it home,
    protect it.
Months later, I find another. If I can find
    one more like
this, and then a tabletop . . . but what
    then? If I only had
real tools, not just rocks to pound my
    bent, rusty nails. Father sold
his tools thinking he'd buy new ones

here, but we've spent that money.
Everyone seems curious about our
    "home," but no one thinks
a young girl would have a use for a
    hammer and a saw. I'm
not sure I would know how to use them if
    I had them — I've been
studying the shipbuilding from a
    distance, trying to learn.
I stay hidden in the trees and watch the
    men haul in the logs —
not once have I seen them stumble. Each
    man has a job to do:
someone sets the log in place; others saw
    it, or strip the bark.
My favorite part is when they raise the
    ship's ribs, one after
another, and I first see what shape the
    ship will be. No one
guesses about cutting; each part is
    "measured twice, cut once," the
way Mother cuts cloth. The shipyard is
    noisy, but the men are
quiet when they're trying to fit the parts
    together. I go
away before they see me, and later watch

them walking home
two by two, or singly, young and old.
What would our life be if
we had Father here? Back home, he
would almost always smile at
me when he came home, and Flora and
Margaret would stop their
play and run to meet him. He'd be
pleased, I think, and proud of us —
Sarah would be too — to see how well
we're managing. Mother
is now sewing piecework to earn money,
and I help her. One
way or another, we will soon take care of
ourselves without
others helping us. Someday others will
ask us for our help.

Beds

When children go to bed, the bed
becomes its own world, holding them
as they drift in and out of sleep.
The solid edges of that world
contain the softer center, hold
the blankets tight. When the child steps
out into the larger world, the
bed holds an almost weightless warmth.

You Will Want to Know
Sarah
Mingulay

Go in. I stand out in the rain, willing
    myself to go inside.
I open the door, look around at everyone:
    Murdo sitting
so still, alone — a helpless expression on
    his face. Grandma has
cooked some whitefish — they must have
    brought it in — Ranald, sitting by the
fire, looks like he wants to be anywhere
    other than here. He holds
a letter — can he read? Does he have
    news of my family? I
straddle *worrying* and *knowing,* as if they
    are separate rooms
inside me. But I must know. Whatever
    they have come to tell us,
it cannot be worse than constant worry. I
    sit down, and in due

course, Ranald clears his throat.
    Grandma sits down beside me and
    picks up
her knitting. Aunt Mairi, Uncle Allan,
    James, and Angus — we all wait
to hear what Ranald's letter holds. He
    looks around, breathes deep, begins.
I have a letter from my brother, Joe, who
    was on the ship with
your family — he writes from Quebec City.
    He tells of tall trees,
wood planks big enough to make houses.
    Oh, I'll just read it. But
when he's read about the trees, about his
    brother, he says, *It's no*
use. He stops. Then goes on: *"You will*
    want to know of the MacKinnons.
It has gone hard for them. The father and
    two of the wee ones —
like angels they were — perished on the
    crossing, of cholera. We
had no way to stop it, as it spread through
    the ship. Findlay had
sold his tools before he left, so Morag and
    the older girl had
money. They hoped it would get them to

*Cape Breton, where they seemed to
think they might find kin. We hear there's
  hunger there. I regret that's all
I'm able to tell you."* The letter goes on,
  but I don't hear. I've
been clenching Grandma's arm. *Which
  wee ones?* I whisper, but we see we've
learned all we will learn from Ranald's
  letter. There's more about the giant
logs — I cannot imagine them, and I do
  not try. What will they
do — Jeannie and Mother — if they *don't*
  find kin to help them? A dog
barks outside; the moon is full. The seals
  are crying on their rock.
After Ranald puts his letter down, the
  room is quiet. One by
one, the women gather round us, softly
  keening for my father —
the strongest, most gentle man — and for
  the "angel" wee ones. Women
are beside me and behind me. I close my
  eyes, lean into them,
go, in my mind, back to the last night we
  were together in our
home. I take the braid from my pocket,

let it catch my tears. *Jeannie,*
if I had gone with you, could I have
helped? I know it does no good
at all to think of that — and I know I'll
always wonder. What were
their last hours together like? What
happened to their bodies? Those of
us who stayed at home must go on living
here without our loved ones.
Mother and Jeannie — and which child? I
want to know! — move on from us,
one day upon another.

Now I look up at
Murdo. He stands,
without his jacket, looking at me gently. I
see, in that same
helpless look I saw before, the strength he
offers. I see his love.

Letters

Holding an almost weightless warmth
(or chill) letters pass from one hand
to another, shifting borders
between the unknown and the known.
Such minute detail: a cricket
chirping by the dam at midnight;
a cracked blue plate. Someone sitting
at a table writing, absorbed in thought.

Have You Asked Permission?
Jeannie
Cape Breton

Inside my sewing basket, I've made a
    pocket for the braid.
Sitting by the fire, I take it out, hold it to
    my cheek. It
has not lost the smell of our old home, of
    Sarah sleeping. And
the smaller braid I made of Flora's hair
    and Margaret's still
holds a soft echo of their laughter, their
    whispers in the dark.
I've made a bench out of a rough plank
    and two large rocks. In the
room here beside it, I want to build a
    simple table for
us to sit at to eat or sew. I now have three
    curved legs; in
due course, I'll find a tabletop. The
    shipbuilders sometimes slice

up round logs, and discard any slice that
    has a knothole. I'm
waiting for one large enough to be a
    tabletop, though I'm
beginning to wonder if I'll be strong
    enough to roll it,
without help, all the way home, on that
    narrow path through the tall
trees. I know Mother won't help: *You
    could be accused of stealing!*
But I see them burn the scrap heap every
    week. I know they have
no use for the things I take. What harm
    can come? Mother says, *The*
MacKinnons have always been honest
    people. We'll not be the
ones to bring shame on our family. Though
    no one here knows us,
we'll behave as we always have. She
    searches my face, asks me,
Have you asked permission to take these
    scraps of wood? I say, *I*
have no idea who I might ask — there are
    so many men there!
To that she answers, *Then, Jeannie, you*
    should not be going there

all alone! Things can happen to young girls.
    These are not people
I've known all my life. We're strangers here.
    It makes me weary. Will
we be strangers always? Those words:
    Things can happen. Is there a
giant in the forest who will grab me? I've
    watched these men, and
they do not seem dangerous. Mother goes
    on: *You've seen how a*
dog can lie sleeping by the fire one minute,
    quiet as a
rock, and then something rouses it, and it's
    barking or growling
by the door? Be careful, Jeannie. All men
    are not as kind as
Father. I want you — and Sarah — to be
    strong and loving, but
women must learn to be a wee bit wary.
    They must protect
themselves. I recall that farmer and his
    eggs. I think about
our Sarah. I lean on Mother's shoulder —
    does she read my mind?
Jeannie, she says softly, *we will pray that*
    Sarah is safe with

good people, who care for her as well as
we would. If only there
were a way to know where she is and how
she is. I have heard
of a school where children learn to read
and write, not far from here.
One day perhaps Willie can go there, and
write a letter from
us to Sarah — if she is still on Barra, I
know it would
stand a chance of reaching her. Until
then, I will trust that this
same sea that breaks on our shores also
breaks on hers, and carries
love from us to her and back, somehow
protecting all of us.

Table

A table absorbs written thoughts
(slight indentations in its wood),
and holds within its sturdiness
echoes of the conversations
that go on around it: laughter,
mealtime chatter, words of comfort.
It's part of all the stories, like
the constant kettle on the stove.

Such Immense Love
Sarah
Mingulay

Braided voices. Quiet conversation in the
    room around me.
It sounds just the same as it always has.
    Grandma Peggy's low voice,
and Aunt Mairi's higher one, talking
    calmly as they drink tea. I'm
still not certain of what happened last
    night — they know nothing of it.
Darkness, like a shawl around our
    shoulders, pulled Murdo and me
    close.
The birds above us in the evening sky
    circled home, calling out
for one another. Waves crashed onto the
    cliffs below us, and we — kissed.
In love, they say, as if love is a place you
    enter — as if we
slice open time and find a whole new

island inside one moment.
I'm shaken by the strength of this. Does
   what we did together mean
I'm going to have a child? Why did no
   one warn me? I've always thought
it happened after people married —
   though I do remember a
tall red-haired girl who had a baby when
   I was ten years old. *Like*
stealing, Grandma said. It was the man
   she meant, not the young girl, but I
have a feeling she would think no better
   of me — us — if she knew.
(The girl — what became of her?) Murdo
   kept saying, *I'm so sorry.*
The stars came out. A white bird rose up
   from the cliff and flew over
us. Such immense love — even if a child
   is growing now inside
me, why must we be sorry for our joy?
   Now Murdo has gone home.
I hope you'll marry me someday, my darling
   Sarah. (His darling!)
There may be a child, and if there is, I will
   marry you. But if
there is no child now, I'll wait three years,

then come back to ask you.
People may have wondered why he left so
    abruptly. Surely they
will wonder if he does not return! I don't
    know which to hope for —
a baby born to shame and scorn, but with
    Murdo soon beside me
and our entire life stretched out ahead, or
    — what would be more proper —
a courtship when I am nineteen and he is
    twenty-two, and then
a wedding with the hens, the dancing,
    and the piping. Oh, I'm
growling inside, wanting both at once, or
    parts of each. Murdo is
as close to me as my next thought, and I
    can't keep those thoughts away.
But I'm afraid. I want Mother here with
    me. And Father. Who will
protect me if Grandma turns against me?
    What woman can I ask
about such a private thing? Aunt Mairi
    would listen, and I've a
mind to speak to her, but I can't be sure
    that even she would stay
with me if she knew. She may think our

whole family would be shamed.

There's something women here do for
    their husbands that I had never
heard about on Barra — they carry them
    out to their boats. Landing
here is difficult, the sea can be rough, and
    if the men can get
from shore to their boats with dry feet,
    their days at sea are easier.
Would anyone think it wrong that I
    carried Murdo to his boat
this morning? Now I sit by the fire, steam
    rising from my skirt. He
carries the braid I've held deep in my
    pocket for so long. Oh, keep
us, God, protect us, through the storms
    we both may face these coming days.

Kettle

The iron kettle on the stove
sings a low song, deep in its throat.
We pour the substance of the song
into a teacup: *Drink slowly,*
sit awhile, it croons, *remember,*
drink deep, and fill me up again.
It sends its heat into the world
while it holds one still central place.

Over the Ruts and Bumps
Jeannie
Cape Breton

Me? I ask, turning quickly to the man I
    have not seen, the
voice that startles me *(Miss?)* as I search
    through the shipyard scrap heap.
*I'm sorry! I'm not stealing! You'll be burning
    this tomorrow.*
It seems less clear now — am I stealing?
    The man approaches. Up
close I see he is not much older than
    myself. He says, *Look*
out for nails. I didn't mean to frighten you. I
    could nearly
kiss him, I am so relieved that he is not
    accusing me.
We stare at one another, neither of us
    speaking for a
moment. I show him the wood slice I've
    found, four feet across. *I*

mean to make a table, I say, then add, *I*
   have three legs . . . I
thought . . . His eyes widen. He glances
   down at *my* legs! It takes us
a minute to straighten out the
   conversation. Then he laughs
like we have long been friends, and I
   relax a bit, and smile too.
I was afraid my eyes were playing tricks on
   me, he says. *I*
knew someone had been round here,
   taking scraps. He waves away my
Sorry, I was only . . . and goes on: *All day I*
   have been hunched
over my work, staring at the shavings
   curling off the planks.
Inside my head, sometimes I see pictures. I
   might be walking
home and think I see a yellow cat that is
   not there. So — a
darling curly-headed girl, hiding in the
   forest's shadows?
If I am imagining you, let me know. (How
   would I?) *If*
you would like my help, I'm at your service.
   He gives a little bow.

*They'll never miss this — you are right
     about that.* I hesitate
for just a moment — he's a stranger —
     Mother's words come back to
me — *Be a wee bit wary* — but it's so
     clear that I need help.
Proper or practical — how do I decide?
     Yes, I say,
then, remembering my manners, *If you
     would be so kind, sir,
I'm trying to roll this down the trail to
     my . . . home.* He asks, *Where
is your home? I'm John Morrison. What's
     your name?* Could I run
away now? Must I tell him I live in a . . .
     potato shed?
Will he still think I am a "darling curly-
     headed girl"? He
asks again. I say, *I'm Jeannie,* and point
     down the trail.
                              Think of
an otter, sliding down a muddy bank,
     always able to
stay graceful. Now picture me, slipping in
     the mud, sprawling and
ashamed, no one to help me up but this

John Morrison, who
never set eyes on me before today. I have
    not only
landed flat on my back: I can't push the
    tabletop aside!
Get up if you can — he offers an arm. I
    try, shift my weight.
Easy, now. He lifts the tabletop. It rolls
    off, like a strong
boat on a rough sea, over the ruts and
    bumps. John kneels down as
he looks at my ankle, already purple and
    swollen. We
keep glancing down the trail, as the sky
    turns red, signaling the
day's end. It is at least half a mile from
    here to the smooth road.

Trees

Each tree holds one still central place
with its deep roots. Shelter for birds,
squirrels. Branches for climbers, fruit
in its season, and later, boards —
the sweet smell of lumber, fresh-cut,
solidity of wood-made things
(a bowl, a house, a rocking horse).
Shadows of leaves like passing thoughts.

A Long Road, Steep and Rocky

Sarah
Mingulay

The small pinching feeling deep inside
    me. The skirts I've piled in a
heap, so I can loosen their waists when
    Grandma is not watching me.
Tomorrow, I whisper to myself, *a boat will
    come tomorrow.*
Up in the sky, I watch the birds, soaring
    without shame. They do not
look to see if other birds are judging
    them as they build their nests.
Nearly sixteen weeks now since Murdo
    left, promising to come to
me if I send a parcel of feathers for him
    to sell for me —
a request so casual, no one would think
    twice about it. Now
I have the feathers packed and ready, and
    I wait.

Ranald is here.
I go over to Aunt Mairi's house. What
    news does Ranald have for
us? Everyone has gathered. I have
    brought my feathers. Ranald is
laughing at one of Uncle Allan's stories,
    but he stops laughing,
too quickly, when he sees me come in.
    Why? Murdo would not tell him,
(I am certain of it) what happened — yet
    when Ranald looks at me
my face grows hot. I take a deep breath.
    Effie, an old spinster, sits
hunched in a corner watching me — not
    unkindly. I think of those
planks in pirate stories, and have this
    awful feeling, like I am
walking out on one, the rolling sea
    beneath me. I take Effie
a cup of tea and sit beside her, losing
    myself in the soft
shadows at the edges of the room. I hear
    someone ask Ranald
if he has any news, and I think I see him
    close his eyes and
bow his head, as if offering up a small

prayer. Or does he
hesitate to begin a story that he knows
    will bring us grief?

To begin, he says. *The landlords called a*
    meeting. We heard they would
help anyone who chose to emigrate to
    Canada. And they
said we'd be fined if we did not attend. So
    everyone was there.
"Sir" and "madame" at the start. And then
    they started talking about
where we would be going, and when we'd
    leave. At that point, two women
ran from the room, or tried to. A landlord
    stopped them at the door. They
shed bitter tears when they saw they could
    not return to their homes. Then
he — the landlord — told us that the ships
    were waiting. We had no choice!
Of course they had a choice, I think —
    didn't I run off to the hills
to avoid their ship? Anyone could do the
    same! Ranald goes on:
And then — men and women, old folk,
    babes in arms, hundreds of people

105

who woke that morning thought they'd be
asleep in their own beds that night,
only to be on the ships come nightfall. A
few of us pushed them
aside and escaped, but then they got their
ropes and dogs. They threw their
weight against the ones who fought the
hardest, four of them against one
strong man you know — Murdo Campbell
— he was bellowing and crying
as if his heart was torn in half when they
took him on that ship. Now
we all sit here in this room together, no
    one speaking. I feel
the whole room trying not to look at me.
    I see ahead a long
road, steep and rocky. I'm alone. I feel
    the child move within me.

Shadows

Shadows leave our thoughts concealed, hold
shimmering hands across a face
when some slight change in color or
expression would reveal too much.
They protect us from the blazing
midday sun. The comfort of the
oak tree's breezy shade, the solid
sharp-edged shadow of a building.

Outside Our Door
Jeannie
Cape Breton

A table. Willie sitting up and eating
    without our help.
Me — walking again, barely limping now,
    four months since that day.
Tomorrow, I'm invited to John's house.
    I'm happy, but yet
not sure of this. He says, *Mother wants to
    meet you.* But: eagles
nest in trees, ducks nest on the ground. Is
    it best for people, too,
to stick with their own kind? Mother is
    sewing a new dress for
me, but she's not certain either. She's
    seen their home, and even
now that we've fixed up this little place —
    we've made a sort of home
here — we'd not invite such wealthy
    people here.

Much has happened.

For the first few days after I fell, and John
     helped me home, I
was too ashamed to speak to him if he
     came by. Would he not
laugh at me? Thinking I could make a
     table. With no tools? When
he did ask questions, I could see how
     foolish it must seem for
me to think I could make furniture. The
     crude wooden bench that
sits against the wall was one thing, but
     how did I think I'd fit
those three curved "legs" to the tabletop,
     once I got it home? I
am grateful now, though, for all his help.
     The day he and his friend
rolled the tabletop from where it fell in
     the forest, laid it
softly down in the grass outside our door,
     John came into the
room where I sat soaking my sprained
     ankle. He looked all around
and said nothing about our poverty. It
     was weeks before
he told me his father owned the shipyard.

When I spoke of the
grief we suffered on the crossing, he
    listened quietly. Then,
Would you like to borrow my tools to make
    your table, Jeannie?
They're good tools. You could learn to use
    them. Early the next morning,
there they were, outside our door. And he
    was right. I learned enough
about each one, through trial and error,
    to make my table.
Women can do lots of things, I'm finding,
    that people don't think
they can do.
                  Mother finishes the dress
    she's sewing for me,
then has me try it on, and steps back to
    look. *Blue is a good*
choice for you, she says. It reminds us
    both of when we climbed the
hills on Barra, the color of the sky after a
    storm. *Put*
on the scarf that Grandma Peggy wove for
    you. When you meet new
people, it's good to have something familiar
    with you. That last

night with Sarah washes over me. I find
　　the braids, both of
them — mine and Sarah's, and the small
　　one I braided on the ship.
Their smell lingers, all my sisters' hair
　　held in my hand. When my
one brother, here, says — *Don't cry. You*
　　pretty, Neannie, I do start
crying and snuffling until Mother makes
　　me take off my dress.
Now, Jeannie, she reminds me, *remember*
　　your manners. You may
feel shy around these strangers, but they'll
　　see — you're a lovely girl.
Longing for old times pushes me toward
　　tomorrow; inside
me somewhere, a child stops crying,
　　reaches out, and takes my hand.

Tools

With sharp-edged saws, we cut and build,
shaping what we need. A hammer,
handle worn smooth, passed from hand
to hand for generations, drives
new nails into fresh-cut wood. Spin
wool on a spinning wheel, weave cloth
on a loom. Sharpen the scissors,
cut the cloth. Needle pulls thread
    through.

Not Speaking, Not Crying
Sarah
Mingulay

Help me, Mother. Where are you? What
would you say if you were here? All
day I have tried to hear my mother's
voice. She, I know, would not heap
yet more shame upon me. *You should be*
ashamed of yourself. Grandma's
eagle eye, penetrating my most private
thoughts. Aunt Mairi,
too: *For shame. How could you, Sarah?*
Surely you knew better! I long
for just one voice to whisper, *It will be all*
right. But will it? If
even Grandma is ashamed (*Your father*
would be too, she said), what
home do I have? The pony, Lair Ghlas, is
also growing large. It
happened last summer; this is her first
foal. She brings me some comfort.

113

I have moved my bed out to her byre — I
    lean my head against her,
not speaking, not crying, hardly even
    thinking, just resting here
when people are so cold. Faithful, my
    little dog, slept out here
for the third time last night, curled in the
    hay with Lair Ghlas and myself.
That takes care of the nights. Days, I
    walk up to the cliffs. My clothes don't
fit me anymore, so now I'm sitting in the
    byre, sewing.

I hear some commotion. Women
    approaching — there's Aunt Mairi's
    voice . . .
friends of hers . . . Grandma. They're all
    excited: *Where is Sarah? . . . Think of*
it! . . . But he's never met her! . . . Mairi,
    she'll never be a beauty . . .
the only chance she'll have. They lower
    their voices as they near me.
. . . around here somewhere. There she is.
    Oh, Sarah, come, we have good news!
Before I know what is happening, they
    rush me inside, plucking

the straw from my hair, fussing over my
    clothes. They sit me down, and
then, as Grandma gets a cloth to wipe at
    my face — like she did to
Jeannie and me when we were small
    children — Aunt Mairi explains: *This*
morning we have had a visit from the
    lighthouse keeper. I've heard
enough right there to understand what's
    going on. From our kitchen
table, I've sometimes looked across the
    water to the next island,
thinking what a lonely life the keeper of
    the light must have. But
me? Grandma speaks next: *He's heard*
    about you, Sarah. That you are a
good girl at heart — we all know that —
    and . . . well, here is the good news:
The lighthouse keeper — Patrick is his
    name — has said he'll marry you!
Put on a clean dress and come to meet
    him. I swallow hard. It is
news, I agree, but how is everyone so sure
    this news is good?
Last night I dreamed of Murdo holding
    out his arms, his eyes so clear.

Of an embrace so loving, it has stayed
　　with me all day. Did his
ship land safely? Has he found food and
　　shelter? Does he still carry
my braid with him, and think of me as
　　often as I think of him?
Start thinking of your child now, Sarah,
　　Grandma says as she smooths the
dress she's holding up for me to wear.
　　She sees from my face that I
may not be as happy as she is. Am I now
　　no more than a
"girl in trouble" who must marry anyone
　　who asks me? Freezing
inside, I let them fix me up and take me
　　to meet Patrick. His
hand. He holds it out to me. I stare at it.
　　I cannot take it.

Cloth

The cloth through which the needle pulls
the thread is woven so tightly
it can keep out rain and sleet. Yet
look more closely — tiny spaces
allow a needle to pass through
without breaking the threads that form
the cloth. Like a solid wall with
a thousand secret open doors.

Ijouse witlj Cwo Doors
Jeannie
Cape Breton

All I want now is to be home where I can
    collapse in a
heap and take off this dress. How could I
    have been so foolish?
Grandma's scarf around my neck was
    small comfort when I saw that
my invitation was not what I thought it
    was. After my
long walk into town, I knocked on the
    Morrisons' front door as
if I had a right to be there — John had
    said, *Come by at noon.*
What made me think he was inviting me
    to lunch? Looking back,
it all feels so different. Even his first
    expressions of
comfort when I hurt my foot . . . not
    friendship, only kindness. *Take*

her downstairs to the kitchen, John, his
   mother said. *I have guests*
here. I'll be there in a few minutes. I got a
   quick glimpse of
"here" through the front door — a room
   far too fancy for someone like
myself — carved table; chairs with
   cushions; a table set for six.
*Don't forget to introduce her to Eliza. She
   should be*
sewing my dress in the back room. John
   led me to the side door.
Voices greeted him, as people looked at
   me — a cheerful group
of women wearing white caps and aprons.
   Oh, you've brought us a
beauty this time, John, one woman teased.
   Did he even look at
me when he joked back, *Don't I always,
   Maggie? That should be no*
news. I wonder if I looked confused. A
   girl about my age,
plucking chickens in the corner, said, *My
   sister got married*
*and they need a new cleaning girl — will
   that be you?* How was I

to answer that? Oh — I have never
  learned to be a stranger!
This was so new to me — a house with
  two doors? Servants? When John
heard the girl's question, he said to me,
  When Mother comes to the
kitchen, she will talk to you about that. She
  says the Western
Island girls from Scotland have always
  proved to be good workers,
but she wants to meet you herself. *I told*
  her I thought you'd want
a job, and she says we can use you. I just
  stood there. Too much
news at once — "a job" (I would be
  paid?); "I thought you'd want" (so,
  John,
you have thought about me?) — but
  something else — was he saying there
is someone else from home here, perhaps
  from Barra? *Those girls — those*
good workers? I stammered, *Who are*
  they? Where do they live? It was
clear he had not thought about this; he
  was just repeating what
his mother had told him. I looked away. I

know my voice can
carry more of what I feel than I wished
  John to know. I told
him I could not stay. *Please tell your
  mother I am sorry for*
the inconvenience, I said as I backed out
  the door. *Goodbye.*

I may regret this later. I may wish for
  paying work, for
a job beyond the sewing Mother and I
  take in. Now this
freezing rain is soaking through my new
  blue dress as I walk home.
His mother. Not John himself. A cleaning
  girl. Not a new friend.
It is some small comfort that I never let
  on what I thought.

Doors

A thousand open doors closing,
a thousand closed doors opening,
so many places, all at once.
Doors slamming shut — the clarity
of that — or the soft click, goodnight,
as a busy day comes to an
end. A stranger's knock, a welcome
friend who enters without knocking.

Not the First Time
Sarah
Mingulay, 1852

A dream of Father: he comes into the
    byre smiling, speaks to Lair Ghlas.
Foolish pony. Did you think we would
    abandon you when your time came?
That foal of yours will be here any day now.
    When I wake up, I feel
my baby kicking hard inside me, pushing
    little fists against me,
as if announcing: *I am on my way.* I'm
    excited. Scared. Around
noon, Effie comes into the byre. *I saw you*
    walking yesterday, out
back of my house. She looks around the
    byre at the cozy nest I've made
of straw and blankets, then peers at my
    face, and doesn't leave. She's thinking,
taking her time. *You've cleaned the byre.*
    Are you and Lair Ghlas expecting

guests? My eyes fill; tears spill over. Effie
     wipes them away, lays the back
of her hand on my forehead. Her old
     hands are gentle; her gaze is deep.
Like your grandma, you are. Did you know,
     Sarah, I was with her when all
six of her children were born? Strong and
     stubborn woman. Don't worry — I'll
be with you when your baby comes. Rest a
     bit now, while you can. When the
door closes behind her, I am not so
     scared. She wasn't part of that
group that tried to make me marry
     Patrick. Later, Effie comes back with
a kettle of hot water, three blankets, and
     some clean white rags. She looks
at me, puts her hands on my stomach,
     nods. *Soon now. And, Sarah, there is*
no shame. It's not the first time a baby has
     been born to a girl your
age. And it will be some years before your
     child is aware you are not
married. I have been thinking the same
     thing. It is my secret hope that
I'll find Murdo, or that he might someday
     come back here, and not be a

stranger to his child. I dream of him
    returning to us, building a
house where we will live together. But
    there is no time for dreaming now.
The baby is coming. Like huge sea-swells
    crashing through the arch on the
western side of Mingulay, pain washes
    over me. Effie says, *It's*
work, Sarah — you can do hard work. I
    push, rest, push. The sun goes down. I
want this to be over. And then, at last —
    A girl! When I hold her, so
much love comes into me, I have no
    words.
                The door opens. It's Grandma.
I search her face as she comes in,
    carrying puffin soup and bannocks.
There's nothing I like better, and I'm
    hungry. Grandma says, *You can't hold*
those bannocks, hot soup, and a baby all at
    once — let me hold her. There
was a time I feared my child would not
    be loved, that my shame would be
    hers.
What I had no way of knowing:
    Grandma, like myself, gazing at her,

can see nothing but beauty and sweet
    goodness. *I'll tell you what I once
told your mother,* Grandma whispers to
    her. *Whatever you need — ask me —
for anything at all.* Then, to me — *Come
    back home now, Sarah.* I nod.
*Goodbye, Lair Ghlas. When it's your time, I
    will come back out to be with you.*
For the rest of the night, into the
    morning, people come by: *I made
this —* a fine-woven blanket from Aunt
    Mairi. From James and Angus
    *(Welcome
home!)* a feather pillow. People are kind
    (or curious). Aunt Mairi's
friend asks, *Have you named her yet?* I
    answer: *She will be christened —* I
    have
thought hard about this — *Murdina
    Morag. But I will call her Jeannie.*

Midwife

She enters without knocking, knows
when she is needed, knows from years
of watching, waiting, when to come.
Her hands have caught and washed and
    held
the newborn so many times she
knows the meaning of each breath, each
cry. As she ties the cord, she holds:
mother, child, pulsing memory.

The Working of the World
Jeannie
Cape Breton

Father would be proud of you, Mother
    tells me. *Of us,* I say. *We*
came here with nothing. Now we have a
    home and enough money to
feel sure we won't starve. Willie looks at
    Mother, at our money, at
me — *What's starve?* I pick him up —
    he's getting chubby — hug him, look
around the room. *It's when you're hungry,*
    and you don't have food. I go
out to my job, thinking about that.
    Grateful for the lunch Mother
made me, the farmer who asked, *Can you*
    plant wheat? I didn't know. *I*
think so, I said. He looked me over: *You're*
    young, you're a girl, but I
expect you'll learn as quick as anyone. It's
    not hard, and I walk

back home each evening with the money
   I have earned. It is enough.
Deep down — enough.
   And now this evening as I'm walking
   home, full of
all this wonder at the working of the
   world, planning a story
I'll tell Willie as he goes to sleep tonight, I
   pass the place where
the trail to the shipyard meets the road.
   And as I'm remembering
that day I hurt my ankle, I see John
   Morrison! He's walking
with a red-haired man. It's been a long
   time since I've seen John. He
looks pleased: *Jeannie, I was just speaking
   of you.* The red-haired man
is staring at me as if he's been looking for
   me all his life.
You're . . . I . . . Are you? Is she? He
   stutters, looking from me to John.
   You're
not . . . he tries again. *Would you be
   Sarah's sister?* And then John speaks:
That she is. He turns to me: *This is Murdo
   Campbell, from Barra,*

a fine builder. He's new at the shipyard.
    Then it's me stuttering:
A Barra from builder? No . . . a builder from
    . . . did you say — Sarah?
Now we're laughing and talking, all at
    once, walking down the road as
the sky splashes red and orange over us.
    Murdo knows Sarah!
It's true — he *has* been looking for me,
    and for Mother. As far as
I can tell, he knew only that we had left
    for Cape Breton — it's
so long ago, that journey. *Sarah went to*
    Mingulay with her
grandma, Murdo says. (*My* grandma, I
    think — I can almost taste her
bannocks!) He keeps looking at my hair,
    takes something from his pocket,
holds it out and shows me — the braid!
    Sarah's half. It is then I know
there is more to this story than I have yet
    heard. *I have one like*
hers, I say. *I know,* he answers, just as we
    reach home. Here's Mother,
her face full of questions. She recognizes
    Murdo. *I recall*

once when Sarah was first born, I was sick. Your mother took care of me, and you came with her. You were so gentle with the baby. He nods slowly, thinking hard. *I remember that . . . a little baby . . . you let me hold her . . . she was so small . . . that was Sarah! Holding her made me feel strong.* He stops; his face turns red. Mother holds out her hand. Welcome — *I was never able to repay your mother for her kindness. Our home here, such as it is, is your home. Will you stay and have some supper?* I invite John, too, to be polite. *No, thank you, Jeannie,* he replies. *I should be going. But may I come again?*

Memory

Childhood memories pulse through us,
alive in blood and in muscle,
drawn forth by words or touch, motion,
smell, color. A cool hand resting
on your forehead, pepper and salt
on scrambled eggs. A well-worn trail
from one safe place to another.
Echoes of unanswered questions.

My Questions Quiet Down
Sarah
Mingulay

We don't want you to leave us, Sarah, but if
     you are certain you must go
to Canada, we'll help you. Everyone has
     said this. I am looking
at the feathers Aunt Mairi has been
     saving for seven years. Then I
look at her, holding my baby, loving us,
     offering to help us
go: *The feathers are yours if you need*
     them.
               Could I find Jeannie and my
mother if I don't find Murdo? How big is
     Cape Breton, and how would
I begin to look for any of them? Here, I
     know what to expect.
I know my life, unmarried with a child,
     will never be easy, yet
walking these paths and hills is now a

part of me. I will always have
enough food here. Grandma's house is
big enough for us. And when I think
of the crossing, I shudder: What if, like
Father and the wee ones, the
story of my life should end there?
                                 I look at little
Jeannie, knowing
where she got her sea-blue eyes, knowing
those eyes will always cause me to
remember Murdo's teasing, his joyful
greetings and our sad goodbyes.
Walking here, in the places Murdo and I
walked together, knowing
he is far across the sea, and I have not
tried to reach him? Or — a
man and a woman, searching for each
other in a strange, vast land? Which
life should I choose? I go to visit Effie
and ask her what to do.

You're certain he wants to marry you? The
question I've not let myself
speak, out loud or silently. I'm flooded
with it now: did Murdo leave
Barra more willingly than Ranald let me

know? Murdo and I were
stuttering with fear the day he left here.
    How can I be certain his
Sarah, I will marry you was what he truly
    wanted? I heard it
as a declaration of his staunch love, but
    perhaps it only meant
Sarah, I know I must marry you. Being
    noble. What were his thoughts
as he crossed the sea? (No one in Canada
    would need to know of me.)

It's late when I leave Effie. The stars are
    out, Jeannie is fast asleep,
her head heavy on my shoulder. In all
    this, the one clear thing: I am
her mother now. One sweet strong fact
    amid all my questions. Deep in my
pocket, where I used to keep the braid, I
    keep one tiny seashell. I
know it was tossed and pounded by the
    sea — yet somehow it stayed whole.
    Be
like that, whatever comes, I tell myself.
    Don't be crushed. Be a loving
mother — alone or with Murdo. All my

questions quiet down, and I
recall something Murdo told me about
his mother. After she died
of a fever, when he was four years old, he
forgot what she looked like.
He remembered only the feeling of safety
that he had as a
baby and small child, when she was alive.
Even now, when I think of
her, he told me, *I can get that feeling back.*
And then he reached for my
hand, held it. He looked at me with that
deep expression — remembering
her, perhaps, or reaching for that feeling
he recalled. He kissed me then —
and that was the beginning of our
Jeannie. *Oh, little one, I'll keep*
you safe. I will try my best to find your
father. If my heart breaks once
again, I will try to protect yours. I will sleep
now on this promise.

Answers

When a question seeks an answer,
the answer may run out, arms wide,
to greet it. Or it may stand off
to one side, watching and teasing
for a while, flirtatious. It may
be unsure of itself, hoping
that when the question arrives, it
earns and holds its own warm welcome.

Walking Home
Jeannie
Cape Breton

Go home! Shoo! I scold the big black-and-
    white dog that stands in my way
looking fierce, barking at me. Walking
    home from working in the fields,
I've been thinking about Sarah. I stop. A
    girl steps out, looks at
us — the dog and me — growling at each
    other. *I've seen you out walking.*
My name is Elizabeth — my friends call me
    Lizzie. This old dog
would never bite you. Come here, Duke!
    He goes to her. *I see why you*
expect the worst, the way he barks, she
    says. I've seen her too, but we've not
yet met. She walks along with me, Duke
    trotting at her side. *How long*
have you lived around here? she asks me.
    Nearly a year, I answer,

thinking, *Can it be?* She's friendly — and
    so is Duke, when he's with her.
The next thing she tells me is: she goes to
    school. *What's that like,* I ask,
knowing how to read and write? She looks
    at me. *You could find out. Come*
to school with me, she offers. I'm too
    surprised to answer. We say
goodbye. *Think about it,* she says. *School's*
    not hard. I'll help you catch up.
Knowing it's possible has me dreaming
    that someday I could send
a letter to Sarah.
                I think Murdo has told
    Mother something
which she has not told me, something
    important about Sarah. Why
do I think such a thing? What could their
    secret be? I keep asking
myself all the questions I want to ask
    Sarah. Does she want to
leave Mingulay and come here? If we
    could save money, and if there
were a way to send it to her, would she
    come? Murdo is saving
his money to try to get back home to her.

But he told Mother
it will take more than a year — she told
   me that much. She asked what I
mean to do with the money I am saving. I
   have so many
thoughts about that — a warm house
   before next winter; shoes for Mother,
me, and Willie; food — and now, this new
   dream — schoolbooks.

                              Just as I fall
asleep, I see — a brief flicker — Sarah,
   holding . . . Margaret? No . . .
Am I longing for what once was and
   cannot be again, or is
my mind showing me what Mother does
   not say? Sarah — scared, yet calm.
I think hard: What we have done this
   year, we can do again, if need
be. Murdo can have the money I have
   saved so he can go home,
love Sarah and, if I am right, their baby.
                              I tell Mother what
I'm thinking. She looks at me like Father
   did the night before he
died: *There's more to you than we've yet
   seen.* Only this time, Mother looks

like she can see it — this strength I begin
    to see in myself, too.

A long talk. We all agree: Murdo must
    return. Mother tells me
of their conversation. *He wants to marry*
    Sarah, and I gave
my blessing. I know she's young, but,
    Jeannie, you will have no trouble
remembering how determined she can be.
    If Sarah is sure,
then I am sure. Father would be pleased. I
    ask Murdo if I might
keep Sarah's braid tonight, so that I can
    weave our hair together
once again. I loosen both braids. In
    Sarah's I find, like a kept
promise, a tiny seashell — round, white.
    At its center, one small star.

Money

Warm in hands that earned it, money
lets people hold the choices they
have made, the promises they've kept.
Look at the possibilities:
possessions, generosity,
recklessness, or safety. Coins pass
from stranger to sister to friend
as clouds pass in a clear night sky.

The Brightest Star
Sarah
Mingulay

Way off in the distance, I see a boat. I've
    been cutting peat in the
fields all morning, with Grandma and
    Aunt Mairi, and we all stop to look
at the boat as it comes closer. When it
    passes the high cliffs, I start
walking, thinking. I've made up my mind
    and I'm ready to leave. Will my
dog, Faithful, think I've abandoned him?
    Will Grandma? Little Jeannie, will
you someday understand why we left
    here? The boat holds two men. We are
not certain who they are, but we know
    whoever comes here has had a
long day at sea. We go down to meet
    them.

        Sarah, are you sure? I don't
answer Grandma — the feathers are

packed and ready, and a parcel of
her bannocks for the journey — but no,
I'm not sure. I wish she wouldn't
ask me. I'm holding Jeannie, and I stand
back from the sea when the boat
comes in; I'm trying to shield her from
the wind. *It's Ranald,* Aunt Mairi
says, and then she grips my elbow — *Oh!
See who has come with him!* I look
up as Murdo steps ashore and strides
toward me. *Sarah! I tried to
send word that I was coming, but* — He
stops and stares at Jeannie. At me.
Something huge and silent holds us and
surrounds us. Uncle Allan says,
*Why don't we get this boat up before we
begin our telling and our
asking — it is clear there will be stories
here this evening.*
        When we go
to Grandma's house, Murdo sees all the
feathers. *I planned to make my way
there,* I say, *to try to find you.* He
shudders. *I'd been working and
saving money for my fare home when I
finally found Jeannie, your*

144

mother, and Willie in Cape Breton. He tells
how they offered to help.
I might have accepted their offer, he says.
Some people are there for
many years, trying to save money. But
before I paid my fare — your
mother and your sister were astounded
when I told them how this all
fell into place — I was asked to be on the
crew of the ship we'd built.
No fare to pay; in fact, they paid me to sail
the ship to Scotland! He
is enjoying himself, telling this. He
reaches in his pocket and
calmly hands me a small pouch, golden-
red-brown, explaining, though I don't
need him to, *Jeannie wove the braids*
together into pouches. "Bring it
home to Sarah," she said. I open the
pouch, and I can see at once
what Jeannie has put inside — a small
braid of three locks of hair: Willie's
(he must have dark curls now),
Margaret's, and Flora's.
                              Tell us what Jeannie
looks like now, Grandma says. Murdo

looks at me and answers, *It won't be too long before Jeannie is the belle of all Cape Breton. But as for me — no one will ever be as lovely as my Sarah.*

Your mother gave us her blessing, Sarah — she spoke for your father, too. Now, may I trouble those with us this evening to give permission for our marriage?

Sure of myself, I stand up beside Murdo. Uncle Allan says, *I might ask what our Sarah wishes, but her smile speaks for itself. Long life together to you!*

I have become "our Sarah" here. Murdo and I kept promises we didn't even speak out loud, that night a brighter star than we could dream of came into us, and we said *yes* together.

Travelers

When clouds part and the night sky
    clears,
stars are fixed points for travelers
moving away from places fixed
in their hearts as home. Going out
and returning (if they do), they
carry gifts and knowledge, pollen
from one place to another, their
part in the world's golden harvest.

Each Stalk Holds All the Sun
Jeannie
Cape Breton

The wheat is ready for the harvest. We
    gather it and tie it.
Look how beautiful it is — each stalk
    holds all the sun it's gathered,
starting with the seeds we planted in the
    soft, rough earth. When I raise
my head and look up to the sky, I see rain
    in the distance. We
will welcome it. Near the shed we've lived
    in, beside a small stream, we
are moving into a real house. With no
    potatoes buried in
a pit outside it.
                Sarah received the
    weaving of our hair. I
don't understand all the workings of the
    heart, but I know something
of what her life has held since I have seen

her. Even my shoulder
would not have been a comfort, had the
    sea not brought Murdo and his
boat back home. They sent a letter, and
    Lizzie read it to us. Aunt
Mairi says Sarah is a good mother — as I
    expected. *She
looks like you, Jeannie, with big feet and
    small hands,* Sarah says. They have
to ask Ranald to read and write and send
    their letters for them. *Tell
me, Jeannie* — Mother asks the question
    I have not raised out loud, she
says she's been talking to Lizzie's mother
    — *should you be going to
our school?* Lizzie has been telling me
    more about it. I want to
go, but I'm trying to save money. Willie
    needs shoes. If there's a
way to make or buy new beds for him
    and Mother, I want to try,
and it would be nice to put curtains in
    the windows of our house.
Your work all summer has been enough,
    Mother says. *I've needed your
help, and you've given it without complaint.*

Now I'm hoping to do
for you what you've done for others. You've
    had a long, hard journey. It's
your time to be young. I'm just sitting
    here, listening to this speech,
all the thoughts Mother has been keeping
    to herself. I think back. I
built this table, found a house, planted
    wheat. What else could I do? *If*
he were here, Mother says, *Father would*
    want everyone to have food,
and after that, he would want someone in
    our family to read,
don't you think? (But he would not guess
    it would be me.) I recall when
it was hard not to take the last mussel
    from little Flora's plate.
Once we were hungry. Now we're not.
    Mother cuts cloth for a new dress.
Willie's clothes (and all our shoes) can be
    mended. I will go to school.

Jeannie, have you decided? Lizzie asks.
    Mother nods and smiles. *I'll*
be right there, I say. I go out and pat her
    dog, Duke, on the head.

For now, I'm a schoolgirl, like Lizzie.
    Maybe someday I'll be a
mother like Sarah, and be happy with my
    baby, but today
I'm cheerful, walking arm in arm with my
    friend to school. Thinking about
marriage is the farthest thing from my
    mind. Well — perhaps not farthest.
I was happy when John Morrison stopped
    by our house for supper.
Life may surprise me in the years to
    come.
                    The tide is coming in.
I look up. A snowy owl soars in and rests
    on a tall tree. The
brightest sun I've seen for months shines
    on, and in, me. As if we're all
together, all our separate islands washed
    by the same deep sea.

Rain

Part of the world's golden harvest
is the rain the earth absorbs when
the sun disappears for days, weeks.
Soft and quiet or torrential,
falling on the fields, the lakes, fast-
moving rivers, shallow creeks — rain
moves through us, becomes visible
as beauty in the world, as strength.

We Will Be Sheltered

Sarah
Mingulay

It has never failed. The earth gives us
    each stone we need, when we
    need it.
Gathering them from the fields, we're not
    sure which will be of use as we
raise the walls of our home one row
    higher. We place one; the next
    appears.
We have one rule: never use the stone
    that's almost right. And the sea —
    when
we were looking for our door, something
    perfect from a sunken ship washed
in. (At least that's what we guess — a
    round glass window in a wide gray
    board.)
I sit outside feeding Jeannie, watching
    Murdo work on our new home.

Something I have noticed as I watch him
    set our stones: Whether he is
shouldering a big stone into place, or
    setting all the small ones with
his fingers, the inside wall is as well made
    as the outside. Sometimes
Aunt Mairi comes by, *Just to watch you
    smile,* she says. For our wedding gift,
she gave us all her feathers — the same
    ones I almost sold — so we will
have a warm bed in our new home. I'll
    put seashells in the windowsills,
tell my little Jeannie tales about them,
    and about our family.
She may never meet her namesake, but
    she'll be told, *Your Aunt Jeannie went
to Canada and learned to read!* Yes,
    Ranald has brought Jeannie's letter
to me — full of news, and: *We have seals
    in a bay nearby. We have found
a place to gather mussels. I've even seen
    puffins on Cape Breton.
Try not to forget me, Sarah. My love,
    Jeannie.* She knows I won't! Our
houses may be too far for us to travel, but
    I will remember.

Your house will soon be ready for a roof,
and it's good thatching weather.
Do you want help with that? Uncle Allan
asks. *Yes,* we answer, *let's try.*
It's not so hard, with the right tools and
enough help. And so, with little
speech but much care, much laughter,
our house is finished with a golden
roof.
I tuck Jeannie into Murdo's arms, kiss
them both, and we go inside.
If winter winds blow in off the sea, they'll
howl outside, but we will have
food in our home, we'll have one another
— we will be sheltered. Grandma
reads the sky, comes to tell us a storm is
on the way. *It may pass by*
when we're asleep, she says, *but there's no*
question we will feel it. Here's a
plate of fish for the first meal in your home.
It's a long time since Grandma
dressed me in Grandpa William's trousers
and let me go to the only
school I cared about: the cliffs, the birds,
the wild sea. She smiles now, and
says,

I dreamed of my grandmother last night.
She had a way of tilting her
head like you do, singing that song to
Jeannie. I put peat on the fire.
A kettle boils for our tea. The storm
breaks on our roof. We're warm
inside.

Today when I cleaned out the byre, I
looked at Lair Ghlas with her foal,
thought
about the morning Effie asked me to help
her be the midwife. The
farthest I could see that day was
afternoon. Then evening came; we ate
supper in the byre, waiting with Lair
Ghlas as shadows gathered round us.
In the morning, there they both were —
Lair Ghlas with her new foal beside
her,
the soft light of the byre bathing them.
Effie had gone home, so I was
all alone with them, holding that quiet
moment in my mind. Like the
sea, it washed ashore, went out, leaving a
braid of seashells on the sand.

156

Notes on Form

I invented a formal structure for this book, derived in part from my admiration of Celtic knots. The structure has three elements:

- Narrative poems, in two alternating voices.
- Praise poems, each of which praises something named in the narrative poems.
- Line lengths based on syllabic counts.

The Braid

The praise poems are braided horizontally. The last line of one praise poem is braided into the first line of the next praise poem.

The last line of the last praise poem and the first line of the first one are braided together.

The long narrative poems are braided vertically. The last words of each line in one narrative poem are the first words of each line in the following narrative poem, sometimes in a slightly different form. In this edition, each line has been broken into two parts. Only the last word of the second half of the line is braided. Where the last word of a line of one poem has no context in the other story, another word in the line is used as the braided word in the following poem.

At the end of the story, Jeannie makes a weaving of the braid, and this is reflected in the form. Images and words from the first two narrative poems, as well as the subjects of all the praise poems, are woven into the lines of the last two narrative poems.

Syllables

In the narrative poems, the lines all contain the number of syllables of the age of the speaker. At the beginning of the story, Jeannie is fourteen, and the lines in her poems are fourteen syllables each; Sarah is fifteen, and her poems are composed of fifteen-syllable lines. By the end of the story, Jeannie is sixteen and Sarah is seventeen, and the lines of their poems are correspondingly longer.

The praise poems are all eight-line poems, with eight syllables in each line.

Notes on People, Language, and Places

People

All of my characters are fictional. I have chosen names that might have been used in the time and place of my story, and many of those names are still common in those places today, but any resemblance between my characters and real people, living now or in the past, is unintended.

Language

The characters in this story would have spoken Gaelic, a language still spoken in many parts of Scotland and Nova Scotia (especially on Cape Breton). The only Gaelic I've used is the name of the pony, Lair Ghlas, which translates as "gray mare."

Most people in that time and place could not read or write.

A few terms will be unfamiliar to contemporary readers. Most can be understood through the context, but two may need further explanation: The "mussel bailiff" was the one whose job it was to see that people did not gather mussels without permission. (Mussels are a kind of edible shellfish that were used as bait in the fishing industry.) "Barking the nets and sails" refers to a procedure used in tanning nets and sails to keep them from rotting. People boiled bark from oak trees and soaked the nets and sails in the solution. (The bark was imported, probably from Spain, as oak trees did not grow on Barra or Mingulay.)

Places

Cape Breton is an island on the eastern end of Nova Scotia, one of the eastern maritime provinces of Canada. Cape Breton's culture is rich and varied, with influences from many parts of the world. The

Scottish/Gaelic influence is an important part of it.

Barra is an island off the west coast of Scotland. The islands of Lewis, Harris, North Uist, Benbecula, South Uist, and Barra, along with numerous smaller islands, comprise the Western Isles, also known as the Outer Hebrides. They are rugged and beautiful, rich in cultural heritage and natural life. Many seabirds nest in their cliffs.

Mingulay is a small island to the south of Barra. People lived there until 1912. In 1977, when I was teaching in Scotland, I spent a summer camping on Barra, and I was given permission to go to Mingulay for one week. The wild beauty of its cliffs and coves and seashells, the mystery of its empty houses, and the sounds of the wind, the sea, and the seabirds have nourished my spirit ever since.

Acknowledgments

I thank Frances Foster for her insights and gentle encouragement, and everyone at FSG for all they do.

I am grateful to the Indiana Arts Commission and the National Endowment for the Arts for supporting my research trip to Scotland, and to the many people who helped me on that trip, and on a trip to Nova Scotia. I name them here, and thank them for their knowledge and generosity, though most of them did not read the book before publication and bear no responsibility for any errors.

Thank you, Lena Callaghan; D. D. and Peggy Campbell; Sandy and Morag Carmichael; Anne Garvin; Mark and Maggie Hudson; Mary Huige; Andrew Kerr; Collette and Robin Mackie; Linda

MacKinnon; Mairi Ceit MacKinnon; Catherine MacLean; Donald MacLeod; Anne and Ranald MacNeil; Iain MacNeil; Joe and Mary Macneil; Morag MacNeil; Rhoda MacNeil; Teresa MacNeil; John Pendrey; Solveig, Richard, and Tara Taylor; Sr. Marie Tighe; and Carol and John Walker.

I'm grateful for the friendship of many careful and honest readers, and for a two-week residency at the Anderson Center at Tower View, in Red Wing, Minnesota.

Jay Underwood, president of the Nova Scotia Railway Heritage Society; the Gaelic College in St. Ann's, Cape Breton; Dualchas Heritage and Cultural Center, in Castlebay, Barra; and the Allen County Public Library in Fort Wayne, Indiana, were all helpful in tracking down information. Of the hundreds of sources of information I used, one was especially helpful: Ben Buxton's book *Mingulay: An Island and Its People* (Birlinn Ltd., 1995).

I thank my large extended family and especially my husband, Chad Thompson, and our children, Lloyd and Glen. The bagpipes you hear throughout the book are Chad's.

About the Author

Helen Frost's great-great-grandparents emigrated from Scotland to Canada in the mid-1800s. In 1977, she camped for a week on Mingulay, a small island in the Outer Hebrides where much of this story is set. She is the author of *Keesha's House* and *Spinning Through the Universe,* as well as a book of poetry for adults and many nonfiction books for young readers. She lives in Fort Wayne, Indiana.